More Classics
Romantics · *Moderns*

SOLOS FOR THE ADVANCING PIANIST

Compiled and Edited by Paul Sheftel

All-Time Favorites No. 103

Exclusively distributed in Hong Kong by

TOM LEE PIANO CO., LTD.

Sign of Quality

SINCE 1887

6 Cameron Lane
Tsimshatsui
Kowloon, Hong Kong

CARL FISCHER, inc.

62 COOPER SQUARE, NEW YORK 10003
BOSTON · CHICAGO · LOS ANGELES

Copyright © 1984 by Carl Fischer, Inc.
62 Cooper Square, New York, NY 10003
International Copyright Secured.
All rights reserved including performing rights.
Printed in the U.S.A.

ATF103

ISBN 0-8258-0345-4

Table of Contents

Preface

For any one who likes as I do to play "desert island" games — what books, music, records, toys, food, etc. would you want with you if you were stranded on a desert island? — compiling an anthology is a most challenging and yet appealing task. It was indeed in the "desert island" spirit that I set about assembling this collection, asking myself which piano pieces would I choose were I only to include my all time favorites, either from my experience as a student or as a teacher.

But why, some may ask, another anthology with many of the very familiar pieces which are already included elsewhere? To this I can only answer: because these are the classic pieces which are the heritage of every piano student. No compilation which purports to present a cross-section of piano literature could fail to include them.

My first consideration, then, was to try to include the most interesting and appealing examples from the "student literature" for while these books should be welcomed by all lovers of piano music they are primarily intended for the piano student.

Editing has deliberately been done with a light touch. In the cases of the Baroque and Classical examples for which there are few or no original indications, some musical suggestions have been provided; sparingly in some instances, in others, not at all. Edited examples are meant to serve as guidelines for those which are unedited, where students and teachers can exercise their own judgement regarding such matters as tempo, touch and dynamics. I have used Urtext sources whenever possible.

Fingerings have also been provided as sparingly as possible, in most instances only to indicate a change of position. Passages which recur are not fingered, thus obliging the student to recognize the return of a previously given passage, and to finger it accordingly. Fingering is, of course, very personal and students and teachers are always urged to explore alternative fingering possibilities.

The pieces within a given volume are, generally, at a comparable level of difficulty. *Beginning Piano Solos* presents the more elementary level, *More Classics • Romantics • Moderns* the most advanced, while *Classics • Romantics • Moderns* bridges the two levels. Grading, however, can be misleading since seemingly simple pieces can often present obstacles for some students, while so-called advanced pieces often prove to be surprisingly manageable. These classifications, therefore, should only be taken as very general guidelines.

It will be noted that certain composers are better represented than others. This apparent imbalance results from the obvious fact that some composers have been more prolific than others in writing inspired short piano pieces of only moderate difficulty.

In closing, the editor hopes that the many hours spent with these books may be rewarding ones to each of you and that if you should ever get to a "desert island" you may well remember to bring this repertoire with you.

P.S.

Tambourine

JEAN-PHILIPPE RAMEAU
(1683-1764)

ATF103

Passacaglia

from the *Seventh Suite in G minor,* 1720 collection

GEORGE FRIDERIC HANDEL
(1685-1759)

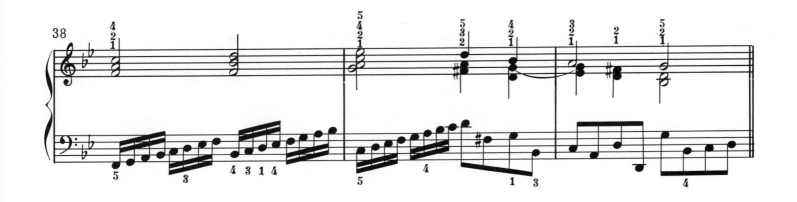

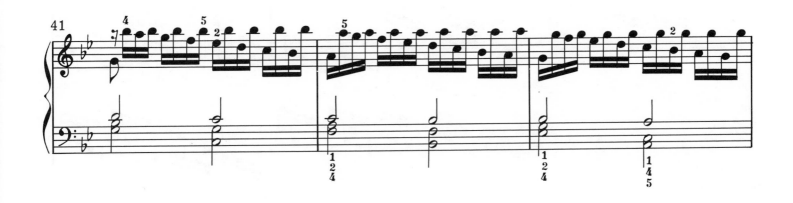

Gavotte

from *French Suite No. 5*

JOHANN SEBASTIAN BACH
(1685-1750)

Prelude

No. 1 from Book 1 of *The Well-Tempered Clavier*

JOHANN SEBASTIAN BACH
(1685-1750)

Minuet

from *French Suite No. 3*

JOHANN SEBASTIAN BACH
(1685-1750)

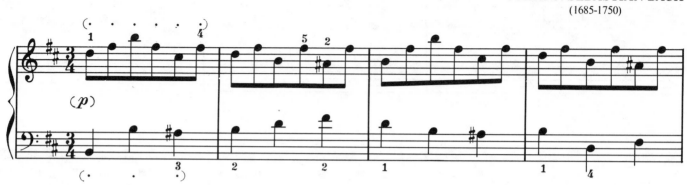

ATF103

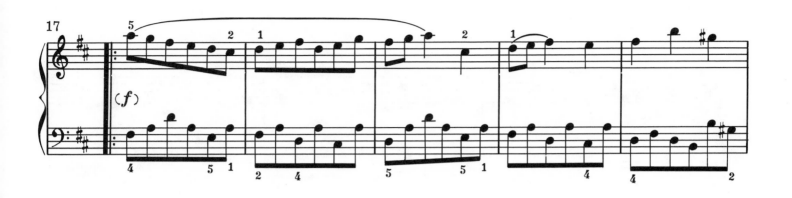

ATF103

Invention No. 8

JOHANN SEBASTIAN BACH
(1685-1750)

Gavotte

from *French Suite No. 6*

JOHANN SEBASTIAN BACH
(1685-1750)

Sonata

DOMENICO SCARLATTI, K.391; L.79
(1685-1757)

Copyright © 1984 by Carl Fischer, Inc.

Sonata

DOMENICO SCARLATTI, K.431; L.83
(1685-1757)

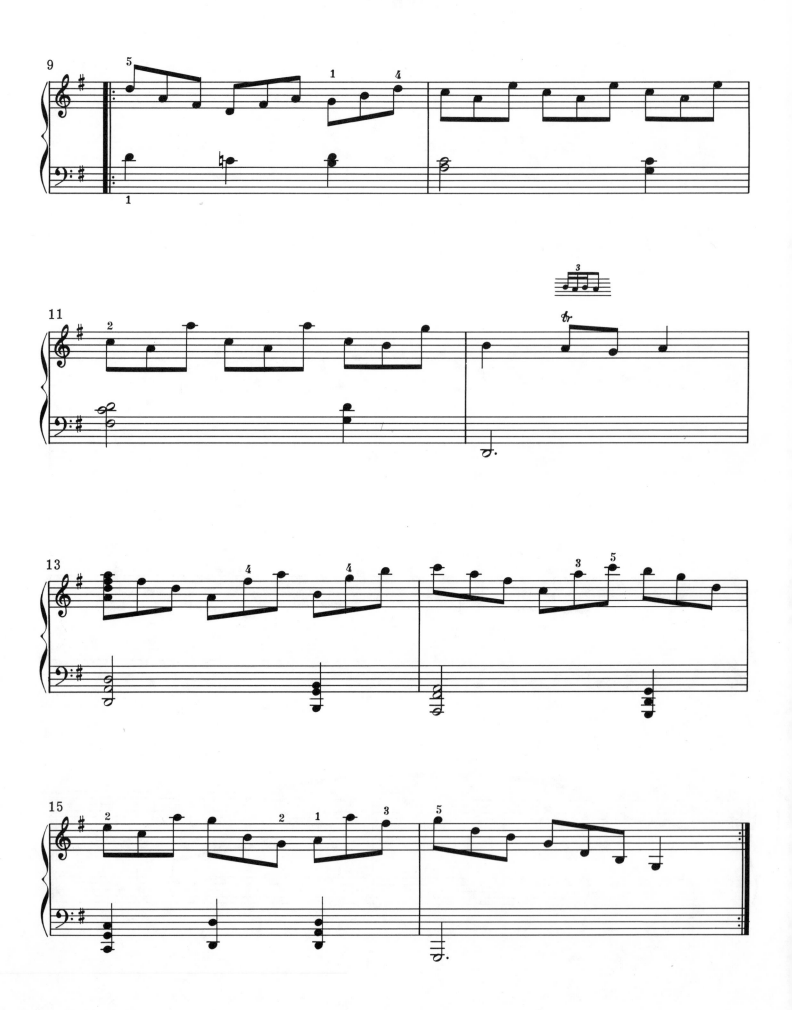

Sonatina

MUZIO CLEMENTI, Op. 36, No. 3
(1752-1832)

I

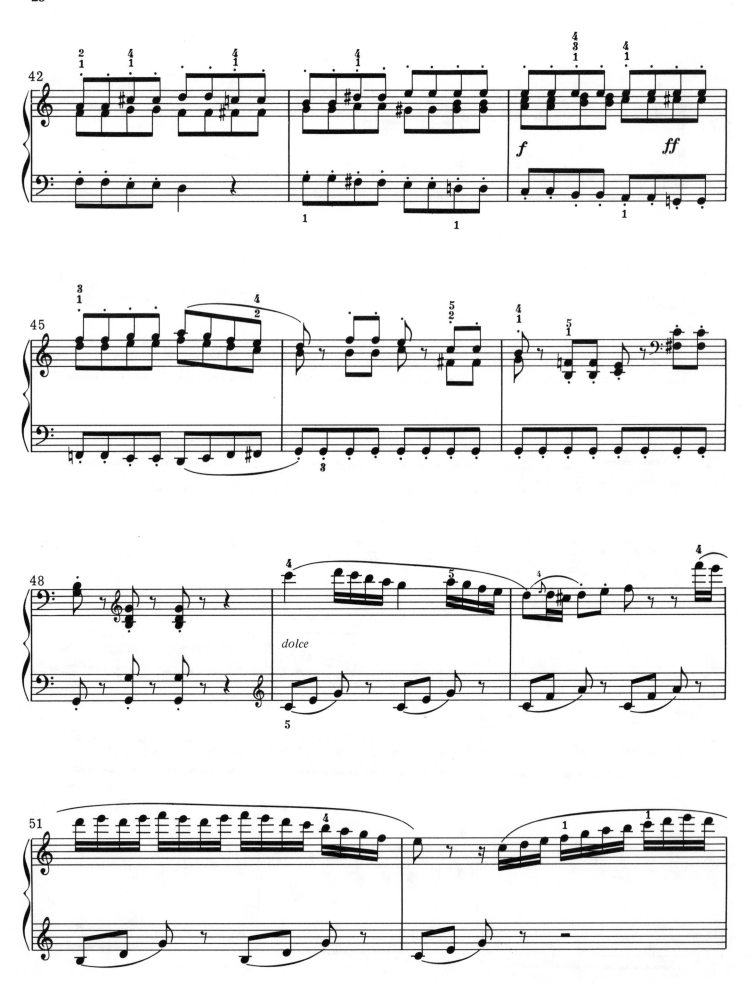

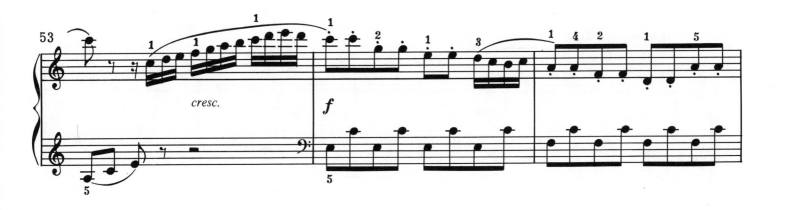

II

Un poco adagio

III

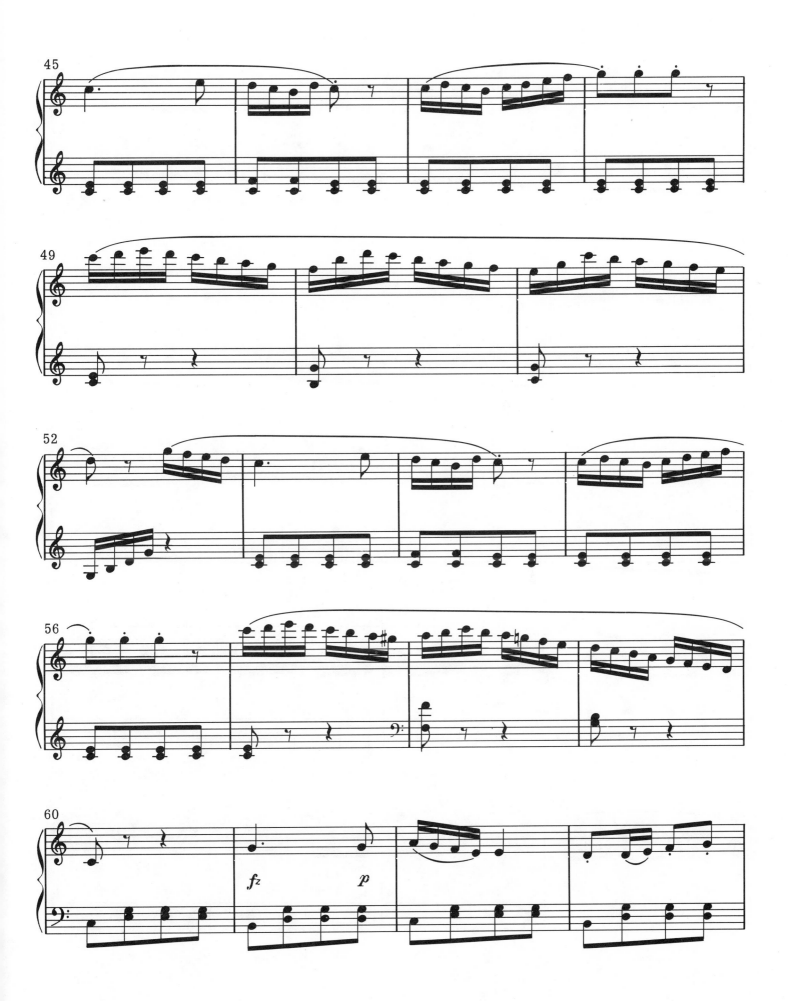

Minuet

WOLFGANG AMADEUS MOZART, K.355(576b)
(1756-1791)

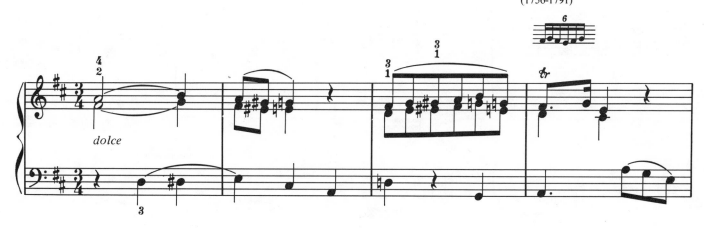

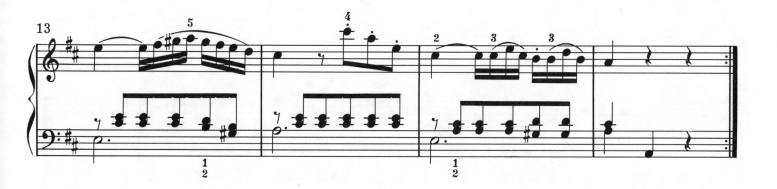

Sonata

WOLFGANG AMADEUS MOZART, K.545
(1756-1791)

I

II

Andante

III

Rondo

Für Elise

LUDWIG van BEETHOVEN, Op. WoO 59
(1770-1827)

Sonata

("Moonlight," 1st Movement)

LUDWIG van BEETHOVEN, Op. 27, No. 2
(1770-1827)

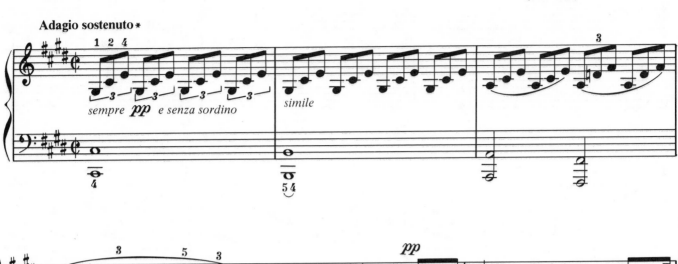

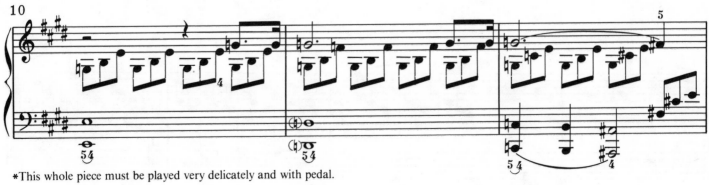

*This whole piece must be played very delicately and with pedal.

Sonata

LUDWIG van BEETHOVEN, Op. 49, No. 2
(1770–1827)

I

Allegro ma non troppo

II

Tempo di Menuetto

German Dance

FRANZ SCHUBERT, Op. 33, No. 1
(1797-1828)

German Dance

FRANZ SCHUBERT, Op. 33, No. 10
(1797-1828)

German Dance

FRANZ SCHUBERT, Op. posth. 171, No. 6
(1797-1828)

Waltz

FRANZ SCHUBERT, Op. 18, No. 1
(1797-1828)

Valse Noble

FRANZ SCHUBERT, Op. 77, No. 1
(1797-1828)

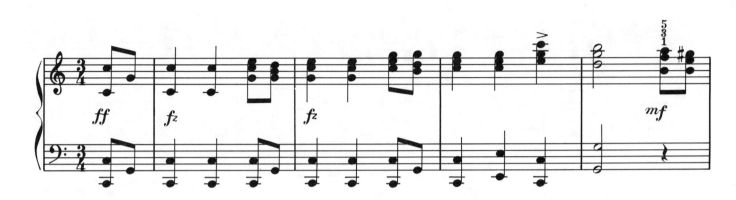

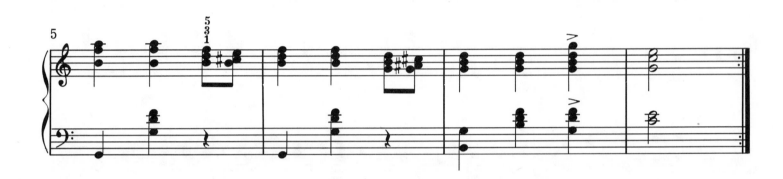

Valse Noble

FRANZ SCHUBERT, Op. 77, No. 9
(1797-1828)

Valse Sentimentale

FRANZ SCHUBERT, Op. 50, No. 13
(1797-1828)

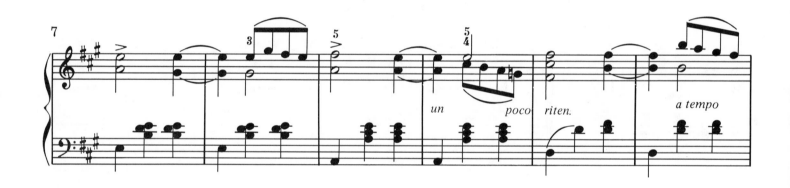

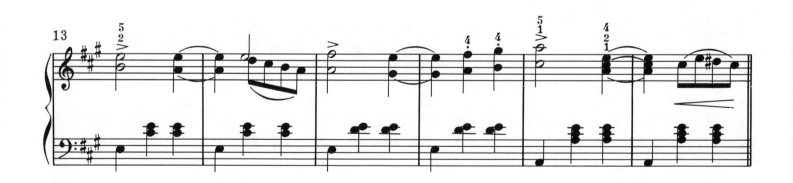

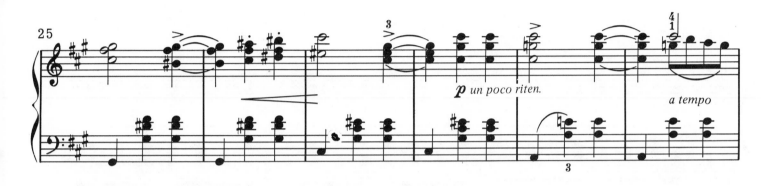

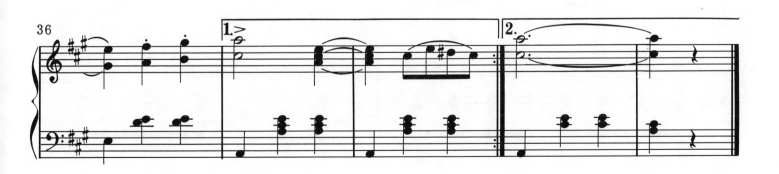

ATF103

Prelude

FRÉDÉRIC CHOPIN, Op. 28, No. 4
(1810-1849)

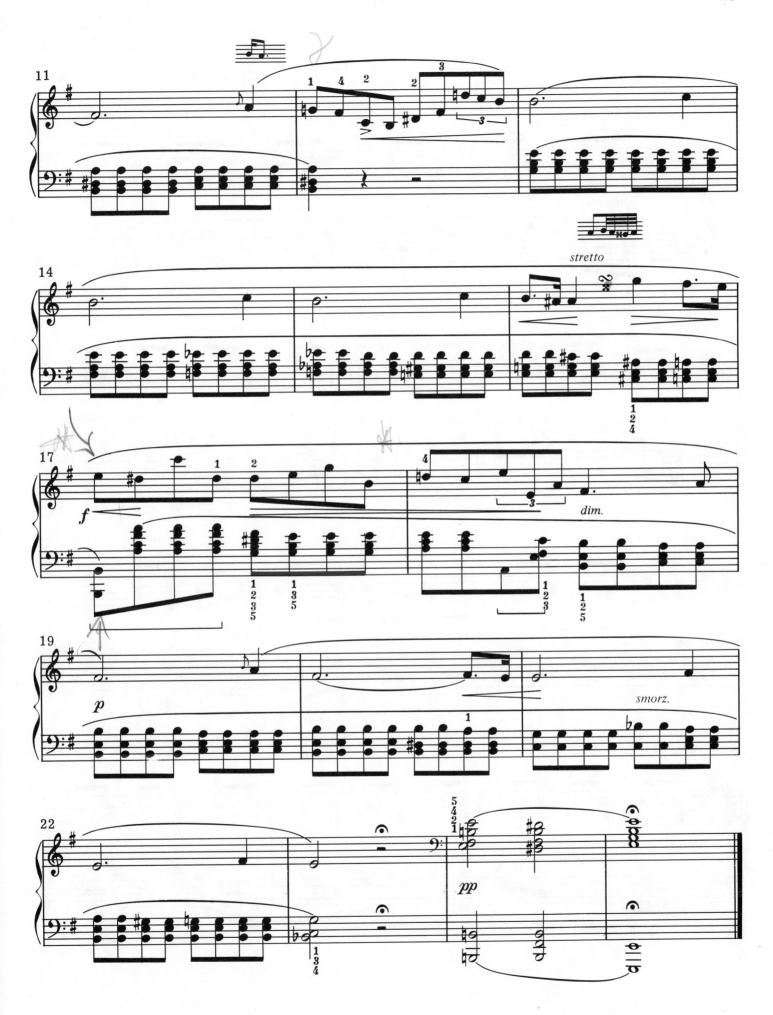

Prelude

FRÉDÉRIC CHOPIN, Op. 28, No. 6
(1810-1849)

Mazurka

FRÉDÉRIC CHOPIN, Op. 7, No. 2
(1810-1849)

D.C. al Fine

Venetian Gondola Song

(Venezianisches Gondellied)

from *Songs Without Words,* Book I

FELIX MENDELSSOHN-BARTHOLDY, Op. 19, No. 6

(1809-1847)

Consolation

from *Songs Without Words,* Book II

FELIX MENDELSSOHN-BARTHODLY, Op. 30, No. 3
(1809-1847)

ATF103

From Foreign Lands and People

(Von fremden Ländern und Menschen)

from *Scenes from Childhood* ("Kinderscenen")

ROBERT SCHUMANN, Op. 15, No. 1
(1810-1856)

An Important Event
(Wichtige Begebenheit)
from *Scenes from Childhood* ("Kinderscenen")

ROBERT SCHUMANN, Op. 15, No. 6
(1810-1856)

Träumerei

(Dreaming)

from *Scenes from Childhood* ("Kinderscenen")

ROBERT SCHUMANN, Op. 15, No. 7
(1810-1856)

Copyright © 1984 by Carl Fischer, Inc.

Frightening
(Fürchtenmachen)
from *Scenes from Childhood* ("Kinderscenen")

ROBERT SCHUMANN, Op. 15, No. 11
(1810-1856)

Fantasy Dance

"Phantasietanz" from *Albumblätter*

ROBERT SCHUMANN, Op. 124, No. 5
(1810-1856)

Consolation

FRANZ LISZT, R.12, No. 1
(1811-1886)

Andante con moto

Copyright © 1984 by Carl Fischer, Inc.

Waltz

JOHANNES BRAHMS, Op. 39, No. 3
(1833-1897)

Waltz

JOHANNES BRAHMS, Op. 39, No. 9
(1833-1897)

Rêverie

from *Album for the Young*

PETER ILYICH TCHAIKOVSKY, Op. 39, No. 21
(1840-1893)

Copyright © 1984 by Carl Fischer, Inc.

Chanson Triste

PETER ILYICH TCHAIKOVSKY, Op. 40, No. 2
(1840-1893)

Allegro non troppo
la melodia con molto espressione

Copyright © 1984 by Carl Fischer, Inc.

Little Bird

"Liden fugl" from *Lyric Pieces,* Book III

EDVARD GRIEG, Op. 43, No. 4
(1843-1907)

Puck

"Småtrold" from *Lyric Pieces,* Book X

EDVARD GRIEG, **Op. 71, No. 3**
(1843-1907)

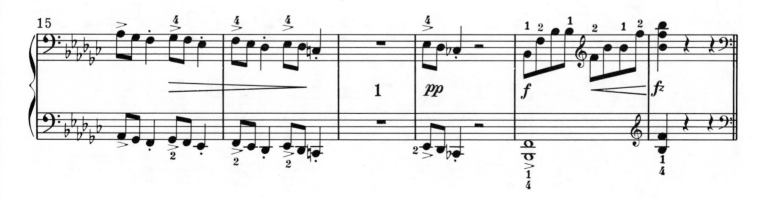

To a Wild Rose

EDWARD MacDOWELL, Op. 51, No. 1
(1861-1908)

Claire de Lune

No. 3 from *Suite Bergamasque*

CLAUDE DEBUSSY
(1862-1918)

Andante très expressif

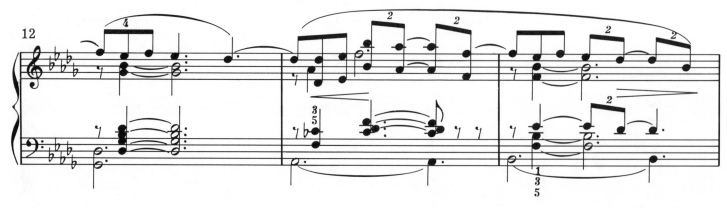

Gnossienne

No. 1 from *Trois Gnossiennes*

ERIC SATIE
(1866-1925)

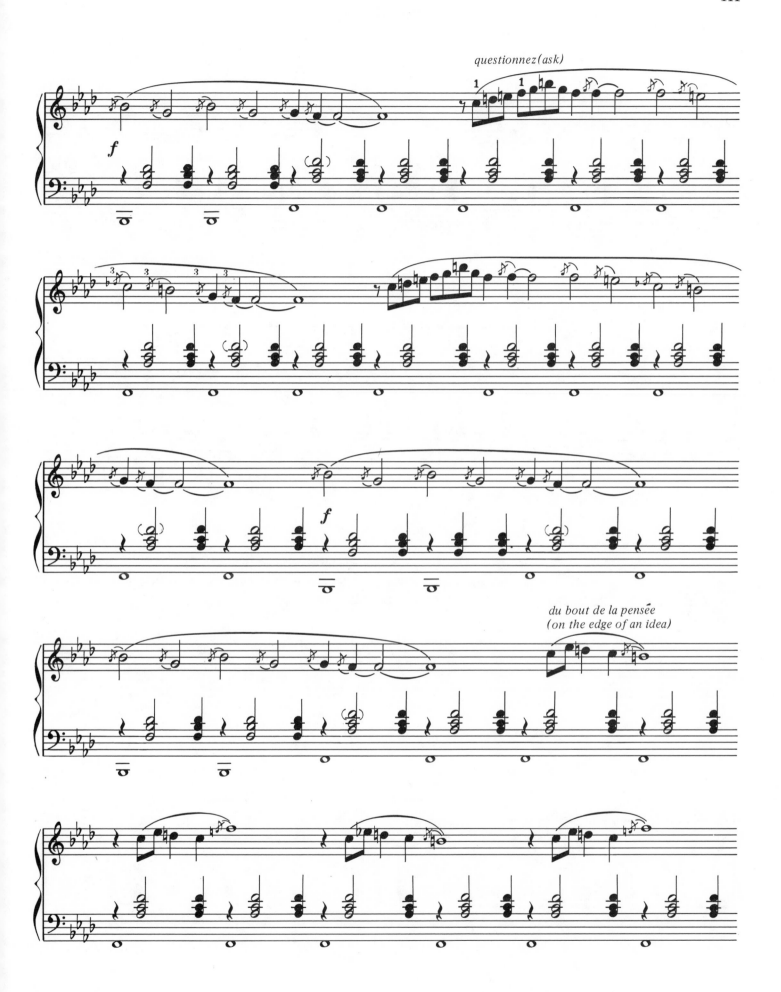

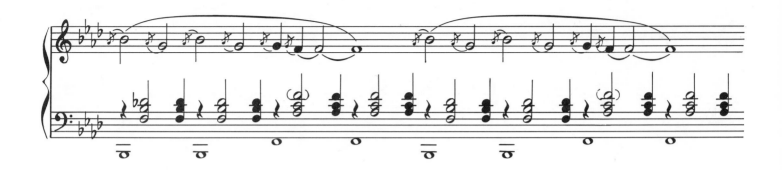

postulez en vous-même
(make your own demands)

pas à pas
(little by little)

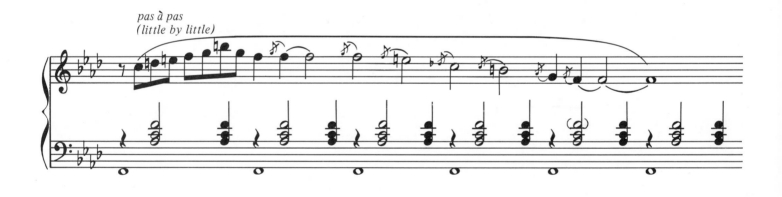

sur la langue
(on the tip of the tongue)

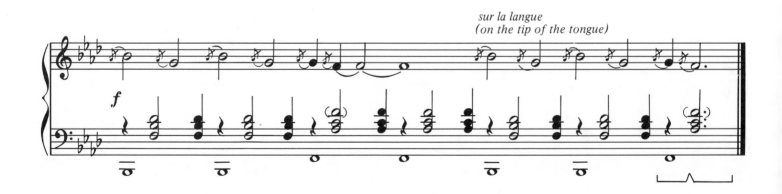

Gymnopédie

No. 1 from *Trois Gymnopédies*

ERIC SATIE
(1866-1925)

Spanish Dance

ENRIQUE GRANADOS, Op. 5, No. 5
(1867-1916)

Andantino, quasi allegretto

Copyright © 1984 by Carl Fischer, Inc.

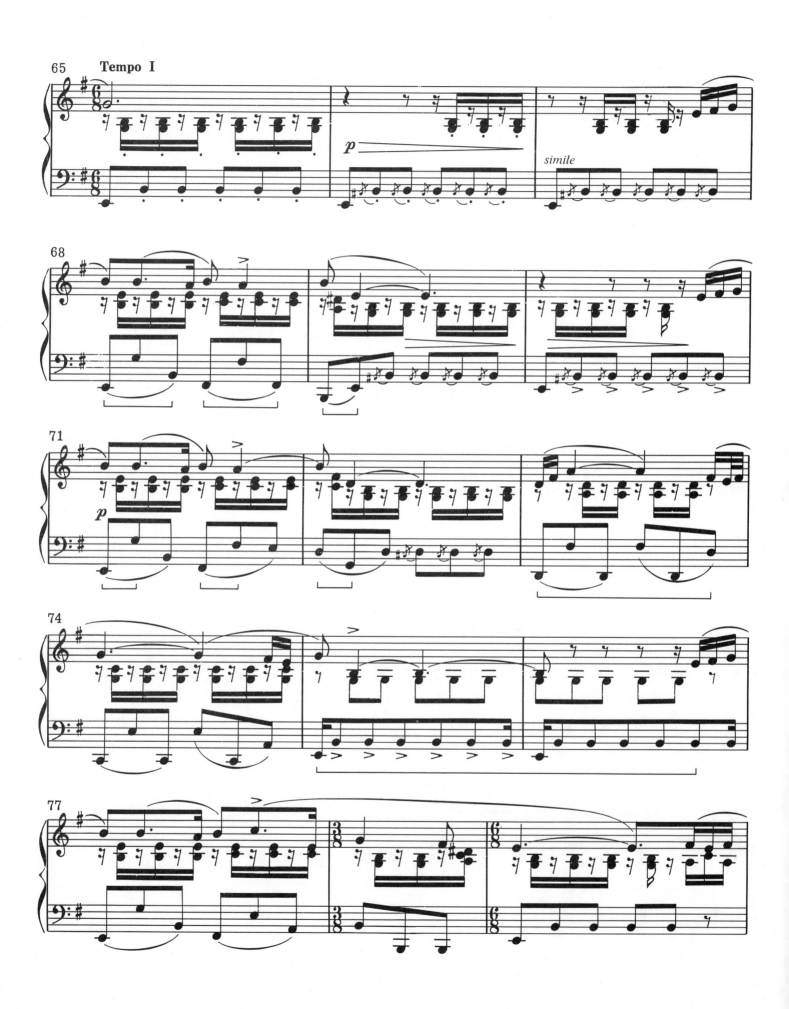

The Entertainer

A Ragtime Two-step

SCOTT JOPLIN
(1868-1917)

INTRO:
Not fast

Bear Dance

No. 10 from *Ten Easy Pieces*

BÉLA BARTÓK
(1881-1945)

Sonatina

BÉLA BARTÓK
(1881-1945)

I
(Bagpipe)

II
(Dance)

III
(Finale)

Kinderstück
(Child's Piece)

ANTON von WEBERN
(1883-1945)

Song After Sundown

RANDALL THOMPSON
(1899-   )

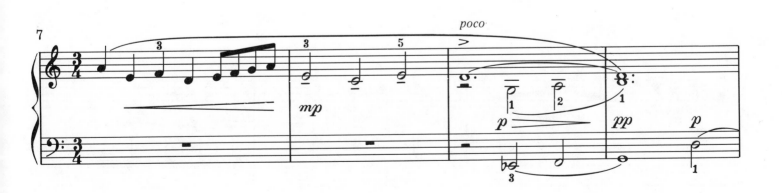

ATF103

Little Prelude

RANDALL THOMPSON
(1899-   )

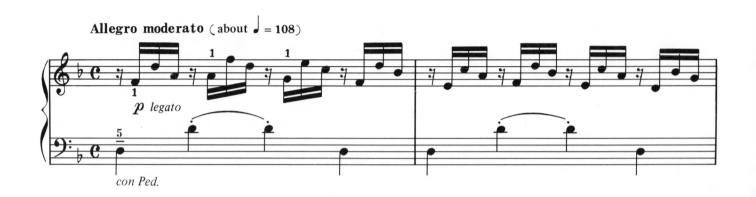

The Young Pioneers

AARAN COPLAND
(1900-   )

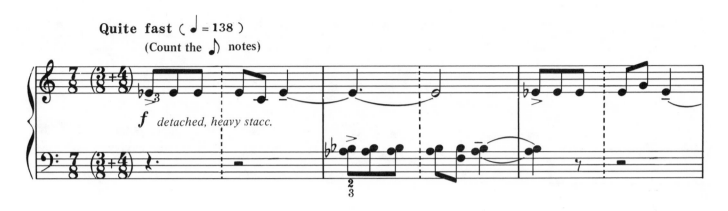

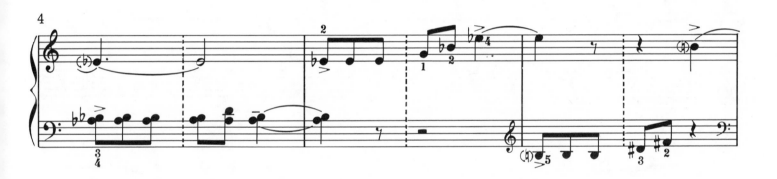

Sonatina

DMITRI KABALEVSKY, Op. 13, No. 1
(1904-   )

I

Allegro assai e lusingando

Copyright © 1984 by Carl Fischer, Inc.

II

III

About Paul Sheftel

Paul Sheftel's multi-faceted career as pianist, composer, author, lecturer, and teacher attests to his versatility and creative musicianship. As a performer, he made his New York debut at Town Hall in 1964 as half of the acclaimed piano duo Joseph Rollino and Paul Sheftel. The duo, based in Rome, performed widely throughout the United States and Europe, appearing in recital and with such distinguished orchestras as the Berlin Philharmonic, Dresden Staatkapelle, Amsterdam Concertgebouw, Royal Philharmonic, Chicago Symphony, and members of the National Symphony at the Kennedy Center. The ensemble also appeared as soloists in the world premieres of Hans Werner Henze's *The Muses of Sicily* for two pianos, chorus, and orchestra and Gunther Schuller's *Colloquy* for two pianos and orchestra.

Since returning to the United States, Paul Sheftel has written two college textbooks (Holt, Rinehart & Winston), a piano method for children (The University Society), and thirteen collections of short pieces (Carl Fischer, Hinshaw Music). His innovative teaching materials, and his engaging personal style as lecturer and workshop-leader have earned him the highest praise from teachers and students throughout the country. Mr. Sheftel is also active currently as a solo performer.

Born of American parents in Como, Italy, Paul Sheftel grew up in Los Angeles where he studied piano with Frances Robyn and Jacob Gimpel, and composition with Mario Castelnuovo-Tedesco. His training continued in Paris, where he studied piano with Lazare Levy and composition with Alexandre Tansman. After receiving his Bachelor's and Master's degrees at the Juilliard School where he worked with Edward Steuermann, he continued his studies in Rome with Guido Agosti on a Fulbright grant.

Records: Deutsche Grammophon